JUNK
RE-THUNK

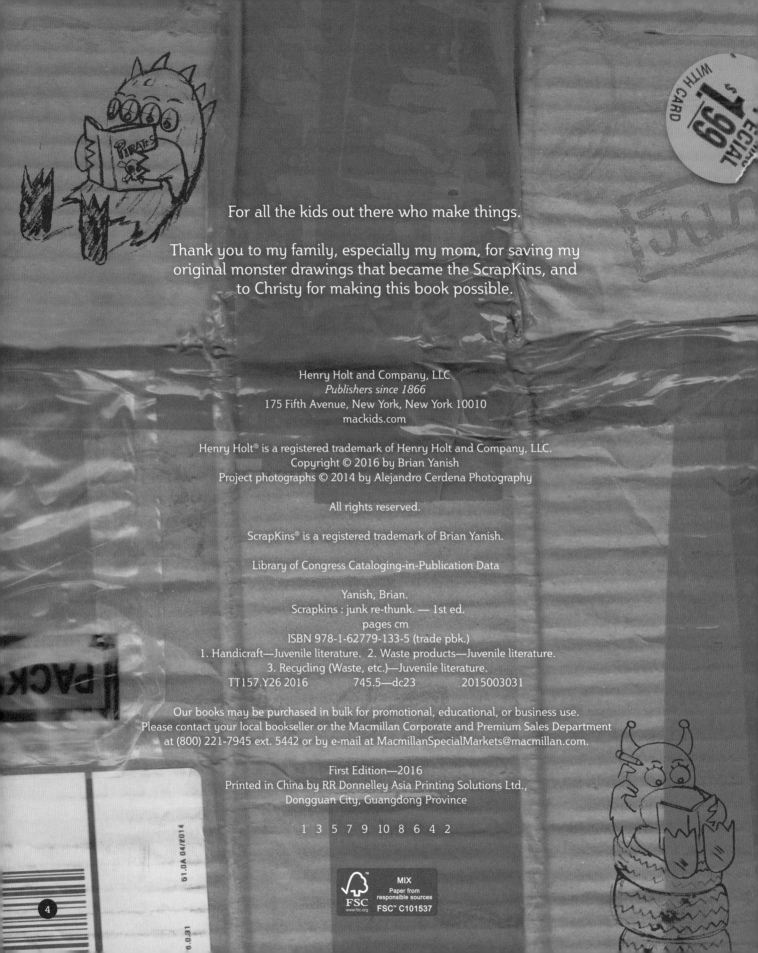

For all the kids out there who make things.

Thank you to my family, especially my mom, for saving my
original monster drawings that became the ScrapKins, and
to Christy for making this book possible.

Henry Holt and Company, LLC
Publishers since 1866
175 Fifth Avenue, New York, New York 10010
mackids.com

Henry Holt® is a registered trademark of Henry Holt and Company, LLC.
Copyright © 2016 by Brian Yanish
Project photographs © 2014 by Alejandro Cerdena Photography

ScrapKins® is a registered trademark of Brian Yanish.

Library of Congress Cataloging-in-Publication Data

Yanish, Brian.
Scrapkins : junk re-thunk. — 1st ed.
pages cm
ISBN 978-1-62779-133-5 (trade pbk.)
1. Handicraft—Juvenile literature. 2. Waste products—Juvenile literature.
3. Recycling (Waste, etc.)—Juvenile literature.
TT157.Y26 2016   745.5—dc23   2015003031

Our books may be purchased in bulk for promotional, educational, or business use.
Please contact your local bookseller or the Macmillan Corporate and Premium Sales Department
at (800) 221-7945 ext. 5442 or by e-mail at MacmillanSpecialMarkets@macmillan.com.

First Edition—2016
Printed in China by RR Donnelley Asia Printing Solutions Ltd.,
Dongguan City, Guangdong Province

1 3 5 7 9 10 8 6 4 2

MIX
Paper from
responsible sources
FSC™ C101537

JUNK RE-THUNK

BRIAN YANISH

Christy Ottaviano Books
HENRY HOLT AND COMPANY
NEW YORK

CONTENTS

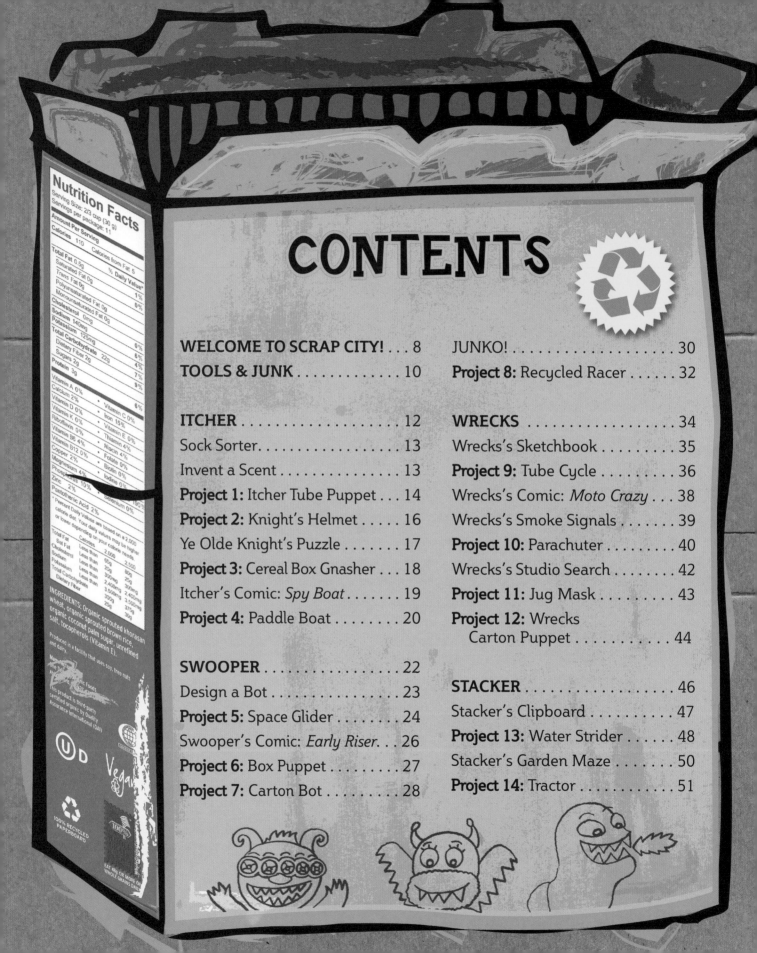

What's
INSIDE!

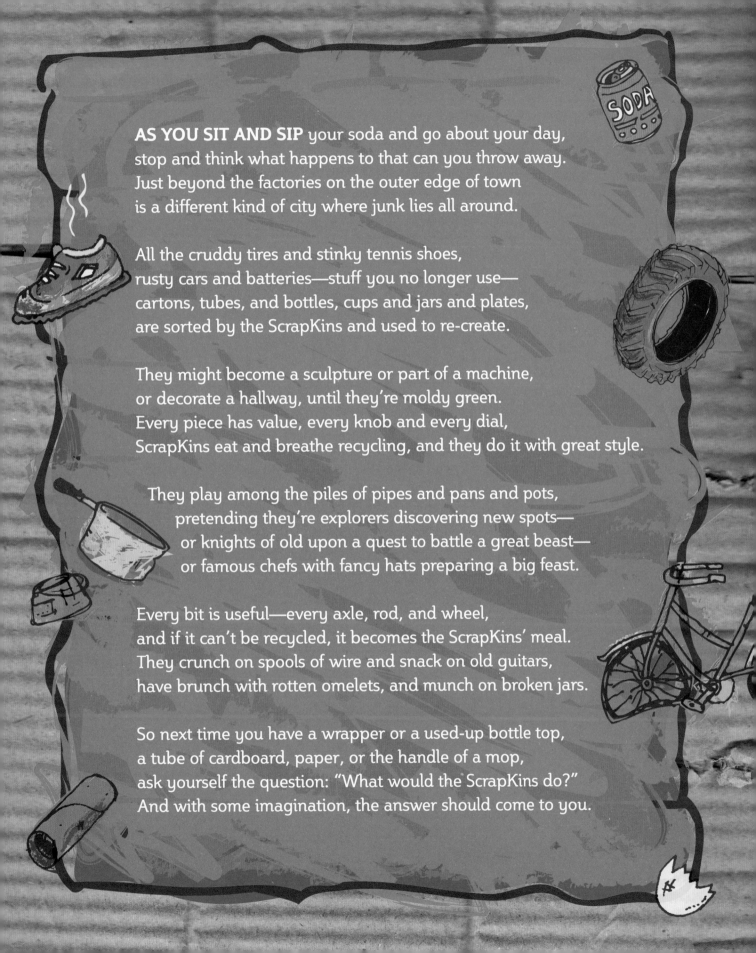

AS YOU SIT AND SIP your soda and go about your day,
stop and think what happens to that can you throw away.
Just beyond the factories on the outer edge of town
is a different kind of city where junk lies all around.

All the cruddy tires and stinky tennis shoes,
rusty cars and batteries—stuff you no longer use—
cartons, tubes, and bottles, cups and jars and plates,
are sorted by the ScrapKins and used to re-create.

They might become a sculpture or part of a machine,
or decorate a hallway, until they're moldy green.
Every piece has value, every knob and every dial,
ScrapKins eat and breathe recycling, and they do it with great style.

They play among the piles of pipes and pans and pots,
pretending they're explorers discovering new spots—
or knights of old upon a quest to battle a great beast—
or famous chefs with fancy hats preparing a big feast.

Every bit is useful—every axle, rod, and wheel,
and if it can't be recycled, it becomes the ScrapKins' meal.
They crunch on spools of wire and snack on old guitars,
have brunch with rotten omelets, and munch on broken jars.

So next time you have a wrapper or a used-up bottle top,
a tube of cardboard, paper, or the handle of a mop,
ask yourself the question: "What would the ScrapKins do?"
And with some imagination, the answer should come to you.

Hole Punch

GLUE

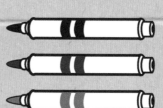
String

Metal Fasteners

Colored Paper

Tape

Scissors

Ruler

Strong Tape
(Masking or Packing)

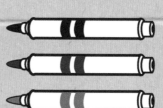
Markers

Waterproof Paints (Acrylic)

Stapler

Paintbrush

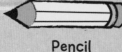
Pencil

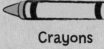
Crayons

TOOLS

What you need to build the projects

JUNK

Rubber Band

Tissue Box

Cup

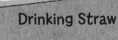
Drinking Straw

Clean & Dry Milk
or Juice Carton

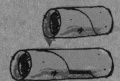
Cardboard Tubes

Plastic Bag

Bottle Caps

Egg Carton

Thick
Cardboard

Plastic Lids

Plastic Bottle

Ice Cream
Sticks

Cereal Box

Paper Clip

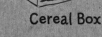

Plastic Jug

REUSE & RECYCLE

All the materials you will need can be found at home. The fun is in reusing things and turning junk into something new and interesting. We call it **"SCRAP-VENTING."**

The more we recycle and reuse, the less we consume and the less ends up polluting our planet.

WHAT CAN YOU SCRAP-VENT?

ITCHER

4 GIANT EYEBALLS

5 HORNS

ABOVE AVERAGE B.O.

EXCESSIVE BODY HAIR

Is that me? Thought I smelled something.

You smell him way before you see him. Hairy, carefree, and home to 127 varieties of extreme body odor, Itcher takes dirtiness seriously. His hairy hide is composed of moldy overcoats and dingy sweaters. Never washed a day in his life—except once, when he accidentally fell into a bathtub.

PRIZED POSSESSION:

World's filthiest sock collection →

CURRENTLY SMELLS LIKE:

Barbecued Toenail Funk, Citrus Sweat Mold-splosion

U.F.S.
(Unidentified Filthy Stain)

MISSION:

Dream it. Do it!
Itcher wakes up each day looking for adventure. He imagines himself a spy, an action movie star, or a famous pirate.

LATEST PROJECT:

Spy Boat
A feature film starring Itcher as Agent Geronimo Carter, who must save the world using his awesome boat. Shot entirely with a cardboard box.

"SPY BOAT"
ACTION FILM
by Itcher

X-4000 →
Movie Camera

FAVORITE SPOT:

Top of Sock Mountain

Foul Beard the Pirate

SOCK SORTER

Itcher's collection needs sorting. Can you find the match for each sock? Draw a line between each pair.

5 WAYS TO SAY "SMELLY"

1. SMELL-TASTIC
2. ODORIFIC
3. STINK-SATIONAL
4. WHIFFISH
5. FUNK MONKEY

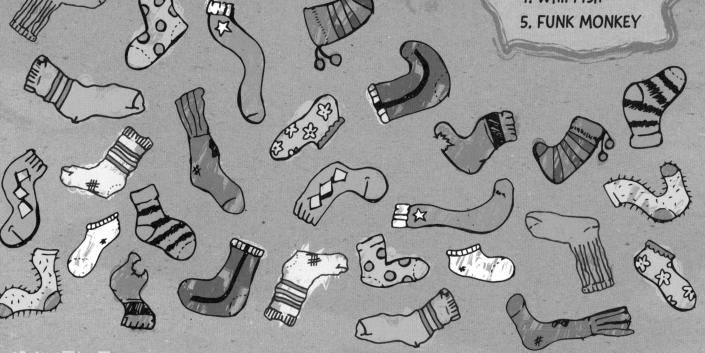

INVENT A SCENT

Choose one item from each list to create some brand-new disgusting scents! Write them on the lines below.

1	2	3
MOLDY	CHOCOLATE	GARBAGE
ROTTEN	HOT PEPPER	WAFFLE
FUNKY	CINNAMON	VEGETABLE
RANCID	SMOKED	BODY ODOR
PUTRID	WATERMELON	SNEAKER
28-DAY-OLD	NACHO	CHEESE
REEKING	SUPER-SPICY	SPAGHETTI
NOSTRIL-BURNING	OILY	PUDDING

SMELL MASTER

NEW

SUPER STINK PERFUME

MY SMELLS:

_____ _____ _____

_____ _____ _____

ITCHER TUBE PUPPET

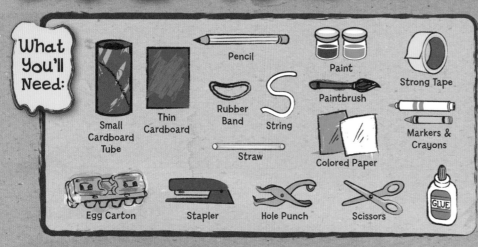

Small Cardboard Tube

Thin Cardboard

Pencil

Rubber Band

String

Paint

Paintbrush

Strong Tape

Markers & Crayons

Straw

Colored Paper

Egg Carton

Stapler

Hole Punch

Scissors

GLUE

1 Flatten tube. Cut out a mouthpiece, starting at the middle of the tube. Save the piece you cut. Unflatten tube.

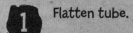

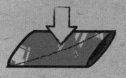

2 Trace mouthpiece onto cardboard. Cut out with scissors.

Glue both pieces together.

3 Staple one end of the string to the mouthpiece. Use two staples.

4 Cut a small piece of straw. Set this aside to use later.

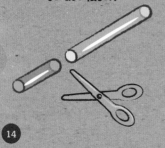

5 Glue one end of the pencil to the **INSIDE BACK** of tube. Use a piece of strong tape to hold it in place until the glue dries.

Glue the small straw piece to the **OUTSIDE FRONT** of tube, at the bottom. Use a piece of strong tape to hold it in place until the glue dries.

6

Take the mouthpiece and turn over so string is on the bottom. Use two pieces of tape to secure mouthpiece to the tube.

7

Make two small cuts in the top back end of tube, across from the mouth.

8

Put one end of rubber band in the small cuts.
Pull the other end out through the mouth and loop it over the bottom of mouthpiece.

Pull the rubber band tight so mouth stays closed.

9

Draw four eyes, five horns, and teeth on paper and cut them out. You can also cut pieces to cover the inside and outside of mouthpiece.

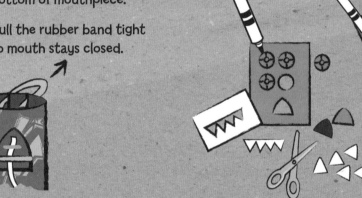
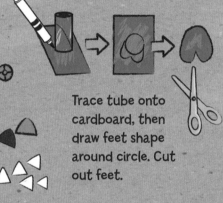

Trace tube onto cardboard, then draw feet shape around circle. Cut out feet.

10

Cut one cup from an egg carton for Itcher's head. Put glue on the top edges of tube and press on the head. Let dry.

Use paints or markers to add some color. Glue on eyes, teeth, horns, feet, and mouth covers.

Use another strip of cardboard to make arms. Glue them on the back of the tube.

11

Put the end of string through the straw. When you pull down on the string, Itcher's mouth will open!

CHALLENGE Can you make the other ScrapKins as tube puppets?

PUPPET SHOW

Use a large cardboard box to build a stage. Write your own story to perform!

KNIGHT'S HELMET

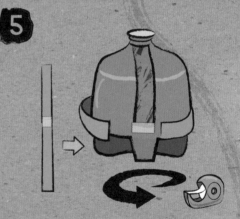

What You'll Need:

Clean & Dry Gallon Plastic Jug

Colored Paper

GLUE

Scissors

Pencil

Markers & Crayons

Acrylic Paint

Paintbrush

Tape

1 Face the handle in back. **Ask an adult to help** cut off the bottom, leaving the back longer and a flap in front.

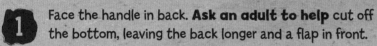

2 Place helmet on head. If the helmet is too tight, cut slits in back flap.

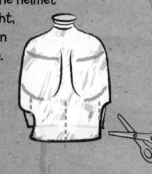

3 Round off any sharp corners. Paint helmet if you like.

4 Cut three strips of colored paper.

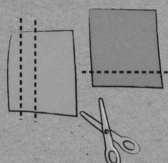

5 Tape one piece down the front of helmet. Tape the other two strips together. Wrap around the helmet, and tape.

6 Draw rivets or cut them out of paper. Decorate your helmet.

Ye Olde Knight's Puzzle

Unscramble the letters to form each word.

Scrap City is full of

J N K U

Itcher's body is covered in

A H I R

Itcher's favorite thing is a

C O S K

You can recycle a metal can and a plastic

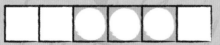

B T L T O E

Itcher's Knight Name:

Unscramble the circled letters to solve the puzzle.

SIR

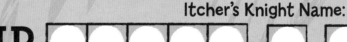

CEREAL BOX GNASHER

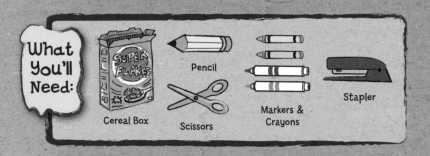
1 Unfold and flatten cereal box.

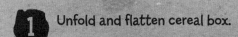

2 Cut off the front or back of the box.

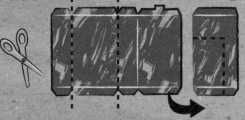

Cut out a long rectangle.

3 Fold rectangle in half.

4 Unfold cardboard. Fold back both corners along a diagonal line.

5 Trim corners with scissors. Use markers and crayons to draw teeth and eyes.

6 Cut out a thin strip of cardboard.

7 Turn over cardboard. Staple one end of the strip at the top.

8 Staple the other end of the strip at the bottom.

9 Slide finger and thumb into loop to use your Gnasher. Open and close fingers to move mouth.

ITCHER IS AGENT GERONIMO CARTER IN . . .

SPY BOAT

"CRISIS ON THE WATER!"

IT'S A TOUGH JOB BEING THE WORLD'S GREATEST SECRET AGENT . . . .

GERONIMO, WE NEED YOU!

THERE'S TROUBLE AT THE MARINA!

OH NO. THERE IT IS!

GERONIMO CARTER HERE FOR SERVICE.

WHAT'S THE CRISIS?

CRUISE SHIP ON FIRE? TIDAL WAVE?

GIANT ROBOT SHARK?

IT'S WORSE THAN THAT!

THERE'S A PLASTIC CUP FLOATING IN THE WATER.

ON IT!

THIS TRASH NEEDS TO BE COLLECTED BEFORE IT HARMS THE SEA ANIMALS!

THANK YOU!!

WELCOME. GERONIMO CARTER NEVER RESTS!

5 MINS LATER . . .

PADDLE BOAT

Clean & Dry Milk or Juice Carton

Rubber Band

Pencil

Stapler

Colored Paper

Scissors

Crayons

Ruler

Drinking Straw

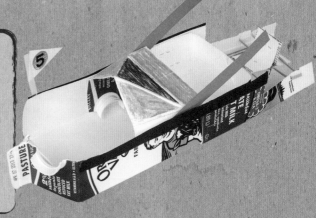

1 **Ask an adult to help** cut the carton in half.

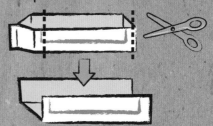

2 Cut off the back end and ¼ of the front end from one of the carton halves. Save these extra pieces.

3 Draw a rectangle on the carton piece, leaving 2 inches at the top. Cut it out.

2"

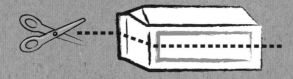

4 Cut the rectangle into four equal pieces. Fold each piece in half.

5 Staple pieces together in a cross formation.

This is the paddle.

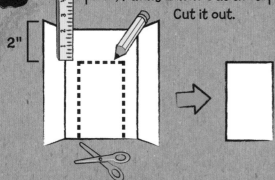

6 Slide the cut piece under the other carton half, just to the edge of the cutout area.

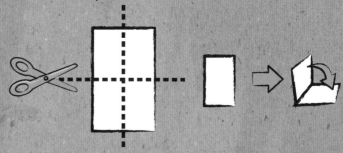

Staple on both sides.

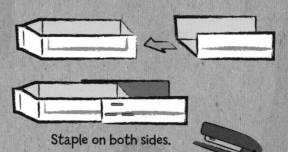

TOP VIEW

7 Cut off a strip from each tail so they are half as high as the boat. Save these pieces.

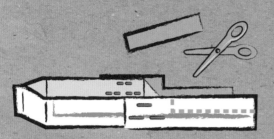

8 Make two small cuts in the tails, close to the ends. ***Do not cut too deep.**

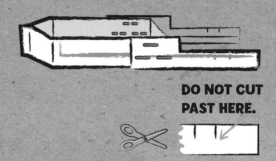

DO NOT CUT PAST HERE.

9 Unfold the extra carton top and turn it inside out. Trim off the front.

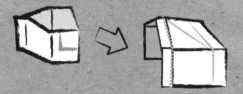

10 Slide this piece into the boat and secure with staples. This will be the cabin.

Slide the two carton strips between the edge of the boat and the cabin.

Use crayons to decorate your boat. You can also add a flag. Use the straw as a flagpole.

11 Stretch the rubber band between the cuts in the tail.

12 Put one blade of the paddle through the rubber band. Twist the paddle back, twisting the rubber band with it. Twist about 20 times.

Keep hold of the paddle. Place the boat in water and let go!

SWOOPER

SOLAR STRUMBULATIONS!

Old carpet | Big brain

Wings made from recycled jackets

TOP FLYING SPEED: 180 knots (207 miles per hour)

MISSION:

Scrap-vent it! If she has a problem and can't find an answer, she builds one!

Part tech-geek, part scientific inventor, Swooper finds it, figures out what to do with it, and then makes it better. A talented car racer, she's the world's biggest Grand Prix Solar Race Fan.

GOOD AT: Speed reading, inventing new words

BAD AT: Telling jokes, using napkins

SWOOPER'S SCRAP-VENTIONS

SOLAR NEST
Swooper's home in Scrap City. Solar panels power the nest's rotation and create electricity.

SELF-COMPLETING HOMEWORK

Homework that does itself. Books that write their own reports, problems that solve themselves.

RESULT: Homework exploded trying to complete a difficult math assignment.

DESIGN A BOT

Help Swooper finish designing Scrap City's newest robot.
Draw a head, arms, and invent some new parts!

BOT NAME:

SPACE GLIDER

U.S.S. COMET

1

Fold sheet of paper in half lengthwise.

2

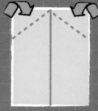

Unfold sheet. Fold down corners to meet in middle.

3

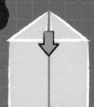

Fold down top point.

4 Fold in half along center line with folds on the **OUTSIDE**.

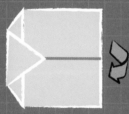

5 Fold down one side, leaving a channel about the width of three fingers.

3 fingers

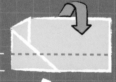

Fold down the other side to match.

6 Unfold. Fold down corners to outer fold lines.

24

7 Fold down **TOP** edge.

8 Refold in half along center line, then refold wings on outer lines.

Fold up edges of wings.

9 Pinch rubber band between front of glider. Place a piece of tape on rubber band to hold it in place. Staple front together twice to secure band.

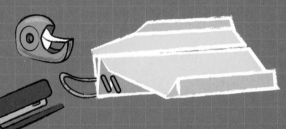

10 Decorate your glider.

11 Cut straw in half.

Place straw piece on top of the **FRONT** of plane. Use a piece of tape to stick it in place.

HOW TO LAUNCH YOUR GLIDER

Loop the end of the rubber band over a pencil, pen, or even your finger. Pull back the end of the glider and let go!

The trick is to keep the band near the top of the pencil so it doesn't hit the top when you release your glider!

HOW DOES IT WORK?

The rubber band creates **FORCE**. With enough force and **SPEED**, the glider counteracts the pull of gravity and the wings cut through the air resistance to make it fly.

The more the rubber band is stretched, the greater the **FORCE** created and the farther and faster the glider flies.

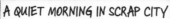

early RISER

A QUIET MORNING IN SCRAP CITY

BOOP!

BOOP!

BOOP!

WHAT IS THAT?

BOOP!
BOOP!
BOOP!
BOOP!

SENSORS DETECT A CHANGE IN LIGHT.

BOOP!

NEW DAY! ALERT.

NEW DAY!

BOOP!

HMMMMMMMM. GOTTA FIX THIS

BOOP!
BOOP!

BRAIN-SPLOSION!

A FEW ADJUSTMENTS . . .

ZIP!

WHIRRRR!

CLANK!

PROBLEM SOLVED.

BOOP-A-DOODLE-DO!

Box Puppet

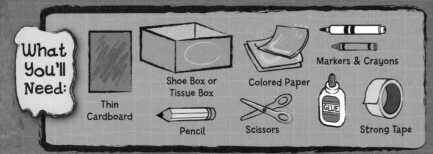

1 If shoe box has a lid, remove it. Cut it off if attached. If you are using a tissue box, cut off the top.

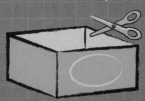

2 Make a cut down the middle of each side of box and bend the two halves apart.

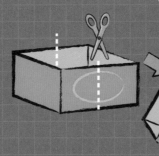

3 Cut two wide strips of cardboard. Fold each strip in half. Fold in half again.

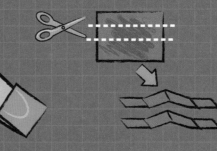

4 Measure where strips will go inside puppet to hold fingers on top and thumb on bottom.

Use strong tape to tape strips into place.

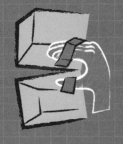
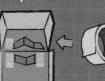

5 Use extra cardboard and colored paper to make eyes, teeth, hair, etc. Design your own puppet face.

6

Glue or tape your parts onto your puppet.

PUPPET STAGE

Write your own PUPPET SHOW!

Use large cardboard boxes to build a stage. Make signs and tickets.

Itcher

Digger

CARTON BOT

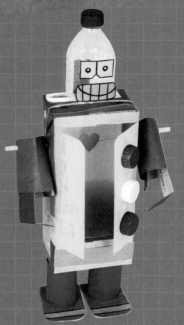

What You'll Need:

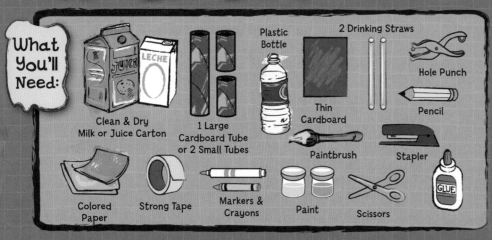

Clean & Dry Milk or Juice Carton

1 Large Cardboard Tube or 2 Small Tubes

Plastic Bottle

Thin Cardboard

2 Drinking Straws

Hole Punch

Pencil

Paintbrush

Stapler

GLUE

Colored Paper

Strong Tape

Markers & Crayons

Paint

Scissors

1

Ask an adult to help with cutting.

If your carton has the angled top, open it up, cut off two of the side pieces, and tape the other two down flat.

2 **Ask an adult** to use a pencil to carefully poke a hole at the top front of carton. Insert scissor tip into hole and cut two doors.

---

3 Flatten tube.

Cut tube into four equal pieces.

4 Unflatten tubes. Punch two holes on opposite sides near the top of two tube pieces.

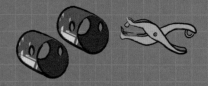

---

5 Cut two long rectangles from cardboard.

Slide one end of rectangle, brown side down, inside tube at opposite end of punched holes. Staple piece so half is inside the tube, half is outside.

Pull out the end that is inside the tube and curl up both ends to form a robot claw. Repeat with other rectangle.

6 **Ask an adult** to use a pencil to carefully poke a hole through one side of the carton and out the other.

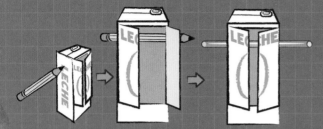

Insert one straw end into the other, then push through the holes in the carton.

7 Slide claws onto the ends of straws. Trim extra straw pieces. Wrap ends of straws with tape.

8 Squeeze plastic bottle flat. **Ask an adult to help** cut off the top or bottom for robot head.

9 Cut a small strip of cardboard. Staple one end inside the bottom edge of head.

Place head on top of carton. Tape or staple the other end of strip to the **BACK** of carton.

10 Cut two rectangles for feet. Glue the bottom of the other two tube pieces on top of feet to make legs. Glue legs to the bottom of carton.

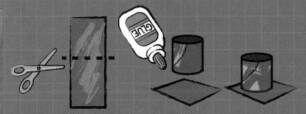

IF YOU HAD A REAL ROBOT, WHAT WOULD YOU HAVE IT DO?

11 CUSTOMIZE YOUR CARTON BOT

⇨ Draw some eyes and a mouth on colored paper. Cut them out and glue them to your bot's head.

⇨ Paint your robot.

⇨ Use scraps, bottle caps, and extras to make knobs and other parts.

⇨ You can even give your bot a heart inside its chest. Tape it to the straw!

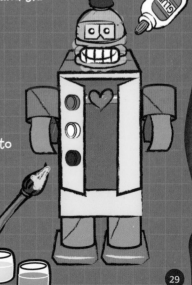

JUNKO!

JUNKO

PLAYER 1

(Pasta Box)	*(Cardboard Box)*	*(Tire)*	*(Wash bottle)*	**Scrap Kins FREE**
Scrap Kins FREE	*(Soda can)*	*(Aluminum Foil)*	*(Grocery bag)*	*(Super Flakes)*
(Milk jug)	*(Juice box)*	**Scrap Kins FREE**	*(Glass jar)*	*(News)*
*(Green You!)*	*(Egg carton)*	*(Memo papers)*	*(Junk mail)*	*(Never Dry bottle)*
*(Water bottle)*	*(Juice carton)*	*(Cardboard tube)*	*(Ketchup bottle)*	**Bring Your Own Bag**

JUNK:
- Newspaper
- Juice Box
- Cereal Box
- Shampoo Bottle
- Scrap Paper
- Milk Jug
- Cardboard Box
- Plastic Bag
- Soda Can
- Egg Carton
- Laundry Soap Bottle
- Glass Jar
- Magazine
- Aluminum Foil
- Junk Mail
- Paper Bag
- Tire
- Water Bottle
- Pasta Box
- Ketchup Bottle
- Juice Carton
- Cardboard Tube

1. If you have a computer and printer, you can download the JUNK CARDS from ScrapKins.com. If you don't, write down each junk name from the list on a piece of paper.

2. Cut out each junk name as a separate slip of paper. Place all the pieces in a hat, bowl, or other container.

3. Pass out a handful of buttons or caps to each player. The players will place a cap on each of their three FREE spaces.

4. One person will be the "Junker." The Junker will pick one slip at a time out of the hat and call out the name of the junk.

5. When the Junker calls out a junk name, the players search their boards to find it and place a cap on it. The Junker keeps picking cards and calling out junk until one player gets five caps in a row across, up, down, or diagonally. The player must shout "JUNKO" to win!

JUNKO

PLAYER 2

RECYCLED RACER

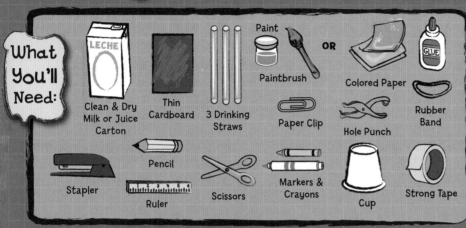

Clean & Dry Milk or Juice Carton · **Thin Cardboard** · **3 Drinking Straws** · **Paint** · **Paintbrush** · **OR** · **Colored Paper** · **Glue** · **Paper Clip** · **Hole Punch** · **Rubber Band** · **Stapler** · **Pencil** · **Ruler** · **Scissors** · **Markers & Crayons** · **Cup** · **Strong Tape**

If you have a computer and printer, you can download patterns from ScrapKins.com. But you don't need them to make the project.

1 **Ask an adult to help** cut carton in half. Each carton will make two cars.

2 Punch two holes on side of carton, close to bottom.

Insert a pencil into the hole and mark the opposite side. Punch holes on that side, using these marks.

3 Trace a cup or something round (about 2 inches across) onto cardboard. Cut out four wheels.

2"

4 Punch a hole in the center of each wheel.

5 Cut two small slits in one end of each straw.

6 Insert cut end of straw through hole in wheel. Fold down the ends of straw.

Staple straw ends securely down. Repeat with other straw.

7 Insert straw through hole in car. Trim extra straw off. *Leave about 1 inch of straw to attach other wheel.

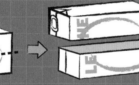

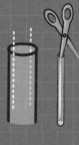

Make two cuts in the end of straw, slide on other wheel, fold down straw ends, and staple.

8 Cut last straw in half.

Slide a straw piece inside each axle.
TIP: If the fit is too tight, cut the straw on one edge so it slides in easier.

9 Design hubcaps and a license plate from colored paper. Cut them out.

10 **CUSTOMIZE YOUR CAR**
Glue on your hubcaps and license plate. Use extra cardboard and carton pieces to add fins and other things. Try painting your car!

FINS

GLUE

EXTRA THICK WHEELS

11 Staple a rubber band to the front of the car, near the bottom.

HOW TO LAUNCH YOUR CAR

1 **Ask an adult to help** bend open a paper clip. Bend up the smaller end so it forms a hook.

2 Tape the paper clip to the bottom of a thick piece of cardboard so the hook end will face up.

3 Turn over the cardboard. Loop the rubber band over the end of the hook, pull back racer, and let go!

WRECKS

SCRAP-TASTIC!

HUBCAPS

FAVORITE BRUSH

BURN MARK

RAZOR TOENAILS

STOMPERS

by Wrecks
Age 6

What's 10 feet tall and shoots fire? Wrecks!

This dino is made from old car parts and sofas. He crushes cars, bends metal bars, and puts it all together to create something amazing and artistic. Clumsy but polite, he'd be the perfect companion for show-and-tell—if he could keep his fire sneezing under control.

MISSION:

Make it Wrecks-cellent!

Take anything you find and turn it into art. Sculpt it. Build it. Assemble it. Paint it. Change it. Squash it. Stretch it. Sit on it. Turn something dreary into something awesome.

I STOMP, I CHOMP, THROUGH RUBBLE I ROMP!

FAVORITE SPOT: Sketching at the Stinky Canal or walking the Scrap Flats to look for interesting pieces of metal.

35 feet

"Recycle-saurus" Sculpture

"Itcher on Sock Mountain"

JUNK BOY

A lonely scientist builds a boy with amazing powers out of junk.

ART
FLAME
ROAR
SCORCH
DINO
CREATE

Help Wrecks find these missing words. Search up and down and sideways!

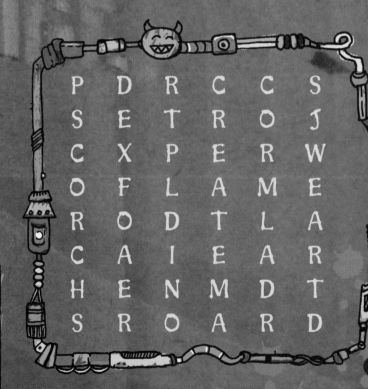

P	D	R	C	C	S
S	E	T	R	O	J
C	X	P	E	R	W
O	F	L	A	M	E
R	O	D	T	L	A
C	A	I	E	A	R
H	E	N	M	D	T
S	R	O	A	R	D

TUBE CYCLE

What You'll Need:

1 Large Cardboard Tube

Cereal Box

3 Drinking Straws

Stapler

Hole Punch

Tape

Scissors

Cup

Markers & Crayons

Paints

Paintbrush

Pencil

Ruler

1 Flatten tube, then cut tube in half along a diagonal line. Each half will make one cycle!

2 Unflatten tube. Cut out a rectangular shape from the top of tube at the flat end. Squash tube down and cut the same rectangle from the bottom.

3 Flatten tube so long sections line up. Cut off the top corner of the front of tube.

4 Punch a hole in the front of tube. Punch a hole in the back of tube just below the height of the front hole.

Use a pencil to make the holes a bit bigger.

5 Trace the large opening of a cup or something round (about 2½ inches across) onto cardboard. Cut out one big wheel.

2½"

6 Flip cup over. Trace smaller end (about 2 inches across) to make two wheels. Cut out.

2"

Punch a hole in the center of each wheel.

7 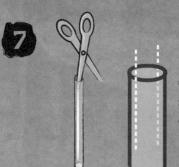 Cut two small slits in the end of one straw.

8 Insert end of straw through the hole in one small wheel. Fold down the ends of straw and staple securely down.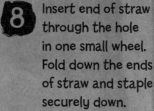

9 Insert open end of straw through holes in back of tube. Trim extra straw off. *Leave about 1 inch of straw to attach other wheel.

Make two cuts in end of straw, slide on other wheel, fold down straw ends, and staple.

10 Cut another straw in half.

Wrap the middle of straw piece with tape, going around 3-4 times.

11 Insert end of straw through hole in the big wheel. Wiggle it until it fits securely in center of straw.

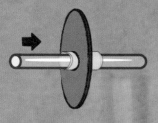

12 Insert end of straw through hole in front of tube, from the inside. Bend the other side of tube to fit remaining straw end through second hole.

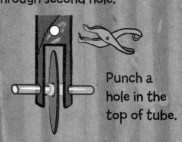

Punch a hole in the top of tube.

13 For handlebars, cut the last straw in half. Cut two long slits in the end of one half.

Bend down the ends and cut one off.

Fold the flap over the other straw piece. Secure with tape.

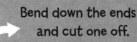

14 Put the end of handlebars into the top hole. Decorate your Tube Cycle!

WRECKS'S SMOKE SIGNALS

WRITE EACH LETTER OF THE ANSWER IN ITS OWN CLOUD.

DOWN:

1. The ScrapKins live in _____.

6. Wrecks grabs junk with his pointy _____.

ACROSS:

2. Wrecks makes art in his _____.

3. Wrecks can _____ cars.

4. Wrecks's Motto: Stomp and _____.

5. When you reuse something instead of throwing it away, you _____ it.

7. Wrecks's favorite thing to do is _____.

PARACHUTER

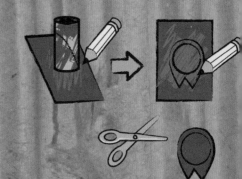

1 Flatten tube and cut a ring from the top about the width of your thumb.

2 Cut open your ring to form arms. Cut out a triangle at each end of arms to form claws, or make little snips for fingers.

3 Unflatten tube. Trace tube onto cardboard. Draw feet shape larger than the tube. Cut out feet.

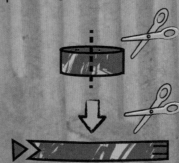

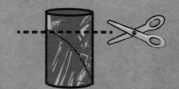

4 Staple arms to back of tube.

5 Punch one hole on each side of tube near the top.

6 Use markers, crayons, or paint to design your parachuter. You can also cut shapes from colored paper and glue them on.

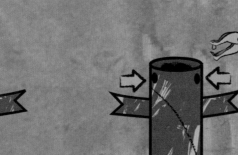

7 Glue feet to bottom of tube. Set aside to dry.

8 Cut the bottom half off plastic bag.

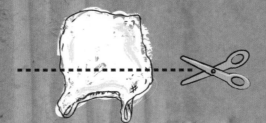

9 Measure two pieces of string, each 24 inches long.

24"

10 Thread the end of a piece of string through one hole. Pull the other end out from inside of tube. Repeat with the other hole and string.

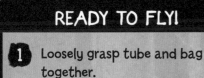

11 Start with one side first. Tape one string end **INSIDE** the bag near the edge at the back corner (A). Tape the other end of string at the front corner (B). Repeat with the other string on the opposite two corners.

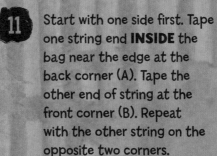

A

B

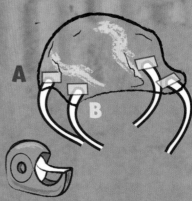

READY TO FLY!

1 Loosely grasp tube and bag together.

2 Toss it in the air or drop it from a high place.

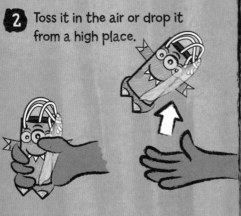

I'm gonna drop my parachuter from Sock Mountain!

HOW DOES A PARACHUTE WORK?

GRAVITY is the force that pulls your parachute back to Earth. The plastic bag catches air and pushes against air molecules to create a pressure called **"AIR RESISTANCE."** This resistance slows the speed at which the parachuter falls.

JUG MASK

What You'll Need:

- Clean & Dry Gallon Plastic Jug
- Colored Paper
- 3 Rubber Bands
- Strong Tape
- Scissors
- Glue
- Paint
- Stapler
- Pencil
- Markers & Crayons
- Hole Punch
- Paintbrush

1 **Ask an adult to help** cut off back piece of jug around the handle.

2 Draw two eye holes with marker. Carefully cut them out. **TIP:** You can cut the jug easier if you pinch the plastic and snip the pinched area to get started.

3 Punch a hole on each side of mask.

4 Use a marker to draw horns, a nose, or other shapes on the extra jug pieces. Cut them out.

5 Staple or use strong tape to attach pieces to the back of mask. **TIP:** Place a piece of tape over the staples on inside of mask to protect your face.

6 Paint or cut out decorative shapes to glue or tape onto your mask. Get creative!

7

TIE HERE

Put one end of a rubber band through the hole, then pull the other end through the loop. Repeat with other hole. Add the last rubber band between the first two. Snip one end and tie them together for your strap.

43

WRECKS CARTON PUPPET

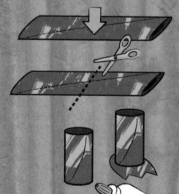

What You'll Need:

Clean & Dry Milk or Juice Carton

Cereal Box

1 Large Tube or 2 Small Tubes

Colored Paper

Paintbrush

Pencil

Paint

GLUE

Scissors

Strong Tape

4 Metal Fasteners (1 inch)

Hole Punch

Markers & Crayons

Stapler

Ruler

If you have a computer and printer, you can download patterns from ScrapKins.com. But you don't need them to make the project.

1 Cut open cereal box. Cut off the back, front, and side panels. Cut the big panels in half.

2

A Draw a tail on one side panel. Cut it out. Flip over and trace onto the other side panel, then cut.

B Put tube on cardboard. Draw a foot shape around the tube. Cut out and repeat.

C Draw two arms and cut them out. Punch a hole at the top of each.

---

3 1¼"

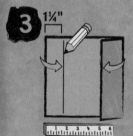

HEAD
A Use a ruler to measure 1¼ inches from the sides. Mark with pencil. Fold edges on pencil marks.

1¼"

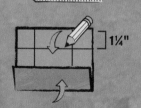

B Unfold. Measure 1¼ inches from the top and bottom. Mark with pencil. Fold cardboard on pencil marks.

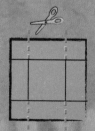

C Unfold. Cut top and bottom as shown by dashed lines.

4 1¼"

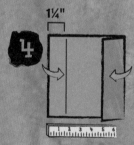

JAW
A Follow step 3A using the last piece of cardboard.

1¼"

2½"

B Unfold. Measure 1¼ inches from the top. Measure 2½ inches from the bottom. Fold cardboard on pencil marks.

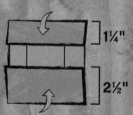

C Unfold. Cut as shown by dashed lines.

5 Flatten large tube and cut in half. Unflatten tube. Glue on feet. Set aside to dry.

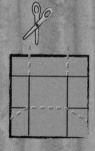

6 **Ask an adult to help** cut the bottom off carton.

Use a pencil to carefully poke a hole in side of carton. Attach arm using metal fastener. Repeat for other arm.

7 Fold head and jaw pieces along fold lines. Fold flaps so they are inside. Staple. Punch a hole in each pointed end of jaw.

HEAD

JAW

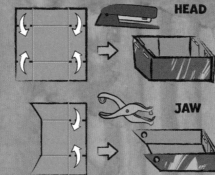

8 Draw two sets of triangular teeth on colored paper. Cut them out.

Tape teeth inside head and jaw.

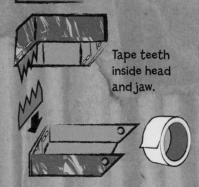

9 Put pointed ends of jaw on **OUTSIDE** of head. Mark holes on head, then punch out. Put ends of jaw **INSIDE** head and attach with metal fasteners.

10 Cut a small rectangle of cardboard from the scrap.

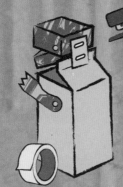

Staple one end of rectangle to outside of head. Staple other end to top edge of carton.

11 Make small cuts in the top of foot tube at front and back. Make two cuts in side of carton, the same width as tube. Repeat for other leg and other side of carton. Slide legs into slots in carton.

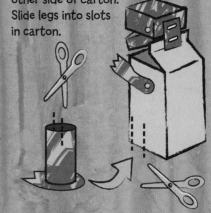

12 Draw a few connected humps on colored paper for tail plate. Cut out.

Sandwich tail plate between the two tail pieces (brown side facing out) and staple.

13 Cut a slit in back of carton and in top of tail. Slide tail into carton until secure.

14 Cut eyes out of paper and glue to head. Paint and decorate Wrecks. Slide your hand inside to use as a puppet!

STACKER

SUPER SIGHT EYEBALLS

SOUND-WAVE-DETECTING HORNS

MOST IMPORTANT CLIPBOARD IN THE WORLD

TAIL FOR DIGGING IN GARDEN

BACKGROUND

MESSY ROOM? NOT HERE! THIS FIVE-EYED BEAST IS A COUNTING, STACKING, ORGANIZING MACHINE. STACKER KEEPS TRACK OF EVERY PIECE OF JUNK IN SCRAP CITY AND CAREFULLY RECORDS IT ON HIS CLIPBOARD.

MISSION: GET IT DONE.

IF IT'S STACKABLE, IT'S TRACKABLE, AND HE'LL FIND WHAT YOU NEED. JUST DON'T KEEP HIM WAITING—HE GETS EASILY ANNOYED.

FACTS

GOOD AT:

LISTENING TO CONVERSATIONS FROM ACROSS SCRAP CITY, WRITING MUSIC, ORGANIC GARDENING

BAD AT:

KEEPING THINGS MESSY, SPORTS

FAVORITE PLACE

STACKER'S GARDEN

SCRAP CITY INVENTORY

Bottles	21,864	☑
Cans	11,201	☑
Jugs	3,242	☑
Bicycle Parts	12,896	☑
Homework	22 tons	☑
Cardboard	13 tons	☑
Tires	1,321	☑
Appliances	986	☑
Newspaper	10 tons	☑
Cartons	3,177	☑
Socks	18,453	☑
Plastic Bags	12,936	☑
Electronics	5,269	☑
Vehicles	394	☑
Shoes	8,793	☑
Styrofoam Peanuts	678,942	☑

DAY:

TUESDAY

OFFICIAL COUNTER:

Stacker

WATER STRIDER

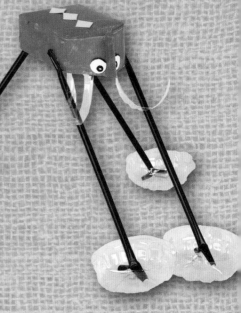

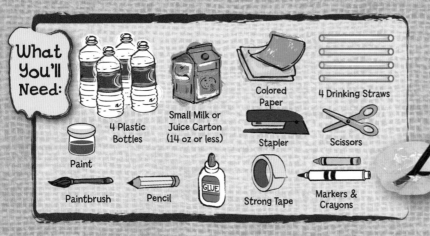
1 **Ask an adult to help** cut the top half off the carton.

2 Flip over the carton half. Paint it brown. Set aside to dry.

3 Cut off the bottoms of the four plastic bottles.

4 Staple one straw on each side of carton near the front. Staple them at an angle so they point toward the front. Make sure the bottoms of the straws line up.

5 Staple the other two straws on the back of carton. Angle them out.

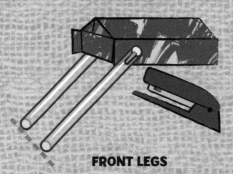

FRONT LEGS

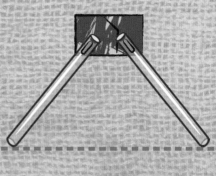

BACK LEGS

6 FRONT LEGS

Cut two small slits in the ends of the front straws.

Make the cuts on the sides so the two pieces bend forward and backward.

7 BACK LEGS

Make cuts so the two pieces bend out to the sides.

8 Cut a piece of tape and roll it up to make a tiny cylinder, sticky side facing out. Place one roll against each straw flap and stick on the bottle bottoms. Press firmly!

TIP: Place your strider on a flat surface and stick on each foot so they are all level.

9 Cut three diamond shapes out of colored paper. Draw two eyes and cut them out.

10 Glue on the diamonds and eyes.

You can cut antennae from the leftover bottle or carton pieces. Tape them inside the front of your strider.

PLACE YOUR STRIDER ON WATER.

HAVE YOU EVER SEEN A REAL WATER STRIDER?
Water striders are insects with six legs that skim across the top of water. Their legs have thousands of tiny hairs that repel water. They use **SURFACE TENSION**, caused by water molecules pulling down on each other, to move across the thin film on top of water.

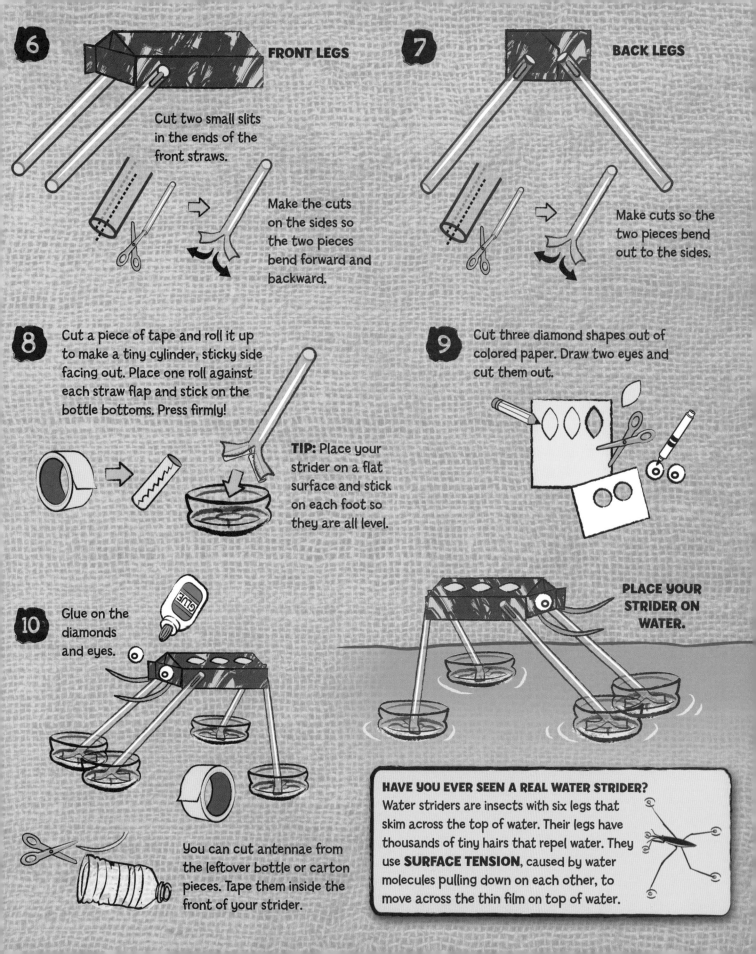

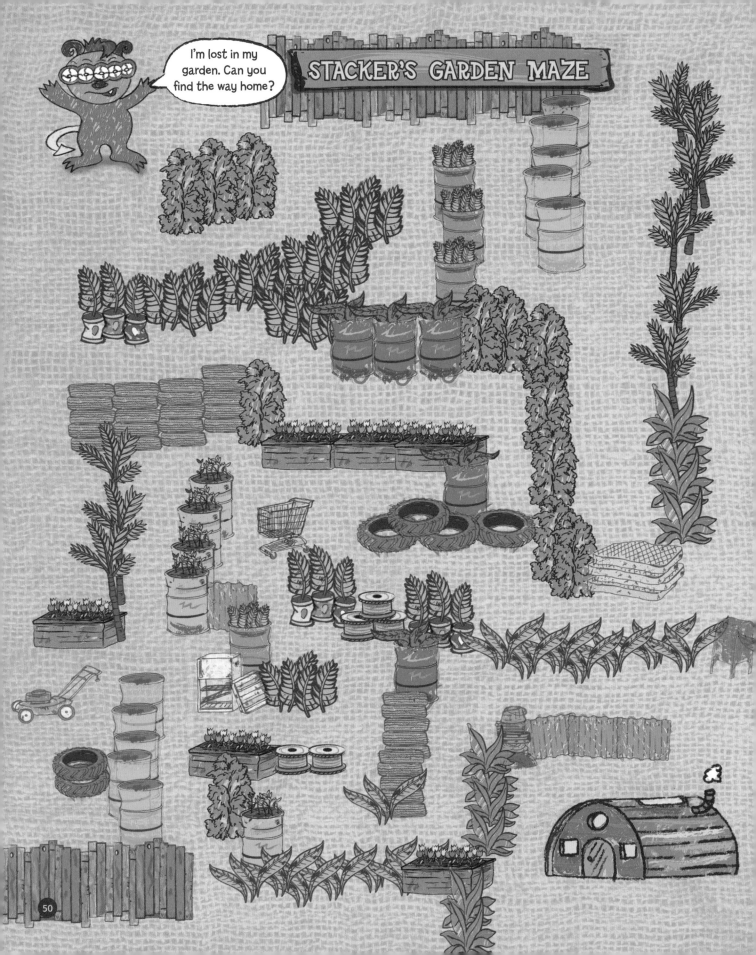

TRACTOR

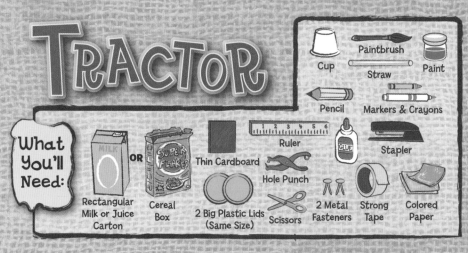

- Cup
- Paintbrush
- Straw
- Paint
- Pencil
- Markers & Crayons
- Ruler
- Thin Cardboard
- GLUE
- Stapler
- Hole Punch
- Rectangular Milk or Juice Carton
- OR
- Cereal Box
- 2 Big Plastic Lids (Same Size)
- Scissors
- 2 Metal Fasteners
- Strong Tape
- Colored Paper

1 Lay carton on side. Measure 2¾ inches from top. **Ask an adult to help** cut off top. Set aside.

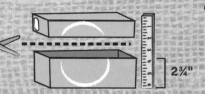

2¾"

2 Trace a cup or something round (about 2 inches across) onto cardboard. Cut out two wheels.

2"

TIP: For thicker wheels, use thicker cardboard or glue two wheels together.

3 Cut a small rectangle of cardboard as wide as the tractor body.

Fold in half lengthwise.

Fold up two outer edges.

4 Tape cardboard piece to bottom front of tractor body.

5 Cut straw in half. Wrap tape once around each end of one straw piece.

6 Use hole punch to make a hole in the center of cardboard wheels.

Ask an adult to help poke a hole through the center of each lid for the big wheels.

7 Wiggle one small wheel onto end of straw until tight. Slide other end of straw through opening in the cardboard and wiggle on other wheel.

8 Use a marker to mark the location of big wheels. *Make sure the bottoms of wheels are level. **Ask an adult to help** poke a hole through both sides of tractor body.

9 Insert a metal fastener through the wheel and tractor. Fold ends of fastener. *Be sure not to fasten too tight or wheels won't turn. Repeat for other wheel.

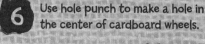

10

A Cut carton top in half. Use one piece as tractor cover.

B Make tiny cuts in sides of leftover piece and fold to form a seat.

C Decorate with colored paper, paints, and markers. Try adding headlights and a grille.

STACKER IN

HERE WE GROW

I CAN USE MY CEREAL MAILER TO SEND A NOTE TO...

MY COUSIN BLINK IN IRELAND!

I'LL ADD A FEW SEEDS FROM MY GARDEN.

Cousin Blin

I'LL TAKE THIS TO SWOOPER LATER.

TIME TO GIVE THESE FLOWERS A DRINK.

A GUST OF WIND...

WHOOPS! BETTER GET THIS IN THE MAIL!

MAIL
PICK UP DAILY

HI, SWOOPER. DID YOU MAIL MY LETTER?

2 DAYS LATER...

YOU MAY WANT TO WATER IT.

WHY WOULD I NEED TO WATER MY MAIL?

YOU'LL SEE.

COUSIN BLI

THAT'S WHAT I CALL A SPECIAL DELIVERY.

CEREAL MAILER

What You'll Need:

Cereal Box · Sheet of Blank Paper · Postage Stamp · Scissors · Strong Tape · Pencil · Markers & Crayons

1 Unfold and flatten your cereal box. Cut off the front or back panel.

2 Cut off the bottom tab.

3 Turn over the cardboard so the brown side is down. Fold up to the bottom of tab.

4 Tape the sides.

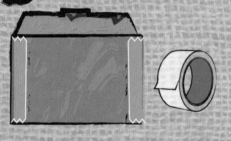

5 Trim the width of your paper so it fits inside the envelope.

*You can also fold your paper if you do not want to cut it.

6 Write a note or draw a picture on your piece of paper.

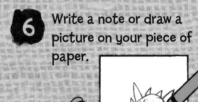

7 Write your address on the front of your mailer in the upper left corner. Write your friend's address in the middle.

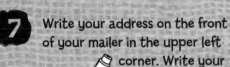

STACKER
25 GARDEN DR
SCRAP CITY

ITCHER
12 SOCK WAY
SCRAP CITY

If you have a computer and printer, you can download a special label from ScrapKins.com.

8 Put your letter inside envelope.

Fold down top flap and tape.

9 You can decorate the outside of the envelope.

Put on a postage stamp and drop it in the mail!

53

CARTON GUITAR

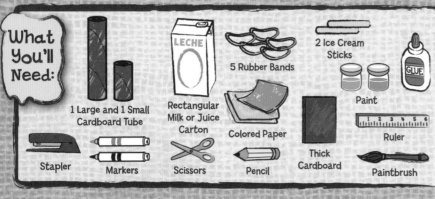

1 Large and 1 Small Cardboard Tube

Rectangular Milk or Juice Carton

5 Rubber Bands

Colored Paper

2 Ice Cream Sticks

Paint

Ruler

Stapler

Markers

Scissors

Pencil

Thick Cardboard

Paintbrush

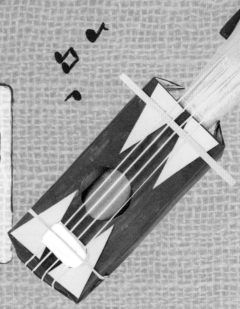

1 **Ask an adult to help** with cutting. Carefully poke a hole in the bottom of carton, then cut a small plus (+) shape.

2 Using a marker, trace around a tube onto the side of the carton.

Use a pencil to poke a hole in center of circle. Insert scissor tip and cut out circle.

3 Push and twist the long tube into the bottom of carton all the way to make the neck.

4 Make two small cuts in the end of long tube and squeeze edges. Put glue on outside of long tube and slide on small tube.

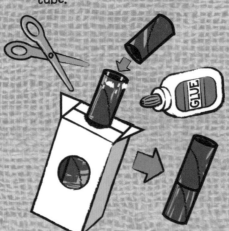

5 Cut a 3x2-inch rectangle out of thick cardboard for the headstock.

6 Cut two slits in top of neck. Put glue along slits and slide in headstock.

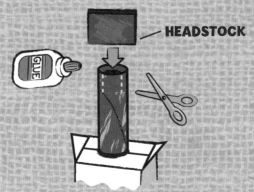

HEADSTOCK

7 Decorate your guitar with markers, paints, and cutout paper designs!

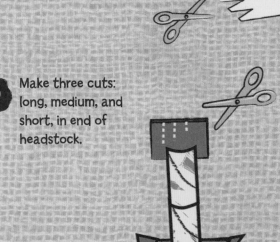

8 Remove plastic spout from carton and glue it on the front, below the sound hole. Open spout.

9 Make three cuts: long, medium, and short, in end of headstock.

10 Stretch rubber bands to loosen them. Put one end in a slot on the headstock and stretch it over the entire body. Put on the four bands, one in each slot, one with no slot.

11 Stick one or two ice cream sticks underneath the strings, between the hole and neck.

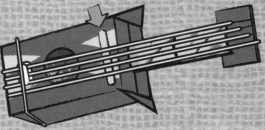

Fold down the top of spout over the strings. Put the last rubber band around the spout.

Play around with the location of the ice cream sticks. Stand one on its side. **Strum the bands to make some music!**

DIGGER

GIGGEROOO!!

How would you like a giant spazzy dog with large teeth that never stops making holes in everything you own? Meet Digger. He digs. Always. Twenty hours a day, you will find him burrowing new tunnels underneath Scrap City. Friendly and constantly covered in mud, no one can figure out how he keeps his teeth so white.

FAVORITE SPOT: The tunnels underneath Grimes Square, where he likes to nap

SCARED OF: Things without holes, bottle caps

BEST FRIEND: Itcher

DIGGER's TUNNEL MAP

HOME

DIGGER TALK:

GIGGEROOO! = LET'S DIG A HOLE!

NOOK = NO

GIBBY = YES

GROBBLEDURG = BOTTLE CAP

BALDBOOG = I'LL BE IN THAT HOLE

GRETCHER = ITCHER

TURGOO = TUNNEL

HOMEGO = HOME

Digger speaks in a language all his own. Most of the ScrapKins have no idea what he is saying.

WELCOME TO DIGGER'S BURROW

Can you spot the 7 differences between the two pictures?

57

SCOOPER

What You'll Need:

- Cup
- Stapler
- 2 Metal Fasteners
- Strong Tape
- Clean & Dry Milk or Juice Carton
- Thick Cardboard
- Hole Punch
- 3 Drinking Straws
- Colored Paper
- Ruler
- Scissors
- Markers & Crayons
- Pencil
- Paintbrush
- Glue
- Paint

1 **Ask an adult to help cut** the carton in half. Paint the half without the plastic spout.

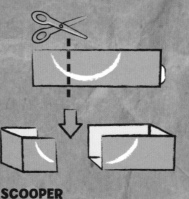

2 Flip over the half with the plastic spout so spout is in the back. Cut off the front third of carton.

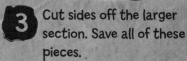

SCOOPER

3 Cut sides off the larger section. Save all of these pieces.

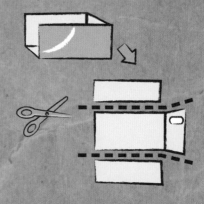

4 Cut off the front of section with the spout to form the seat. Save the cut-off piece.

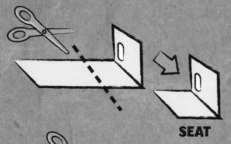

SEAT

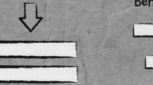

Cut one of the side pieces into two equal strips.

5 Punch a hole in the end of each strip and on each side of the painted carton, near the front.

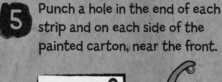

Put the ends of a metal fastener through each hole in the strips, then through each hole in carton. Bend down the ends.

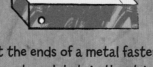

6 Cut the extra piece from the seat into two equal pieces. Fold each piece in half. Fold up two outer edges.

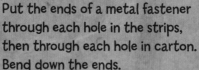

Tape each piece to bottom of carton, one at the front, one at the back.

7 Cut the last carton piece into four equal pieces. Round off the corners.

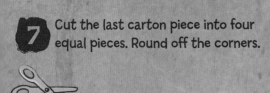

8 Trace a cup or something round (about 2½ inches across) onto cardboard. Cut out four wheels.

2½"

Punch a hole in the center of each wheel.

9 Cut two small slits in the end of each straw. Insert end of straw through hole in wheel. Fold down ends of straw. Staple ends securely down. Repeat with other wheel.

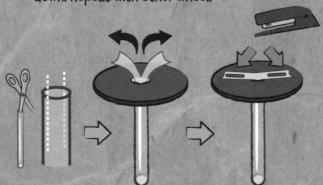

10 Insert straw through opening on bottom. Trim extra straw off. *Leave about 1 inch of straw to attach other wheel.

Make two cuts in the end of straw, slide on other wheel, fold down straw ends, and staple. Repeat for second wheel.

11 Staple the ends of arms to the scooper.

Cut last straw in half. Slide one piece inside each of the axles. **TIP:** If the fit is too tight, cut the straw on one edge so it slides in easier.

12 Use colored paper to decorate your scooper. Cut out a rectangle for a grille and two circles for headlights. Attach with glue.

Put some tape on the bottom of seat and stick inside.

Staple the oval pieces over the straw ends on the wheels.

READY TO SCOOP!

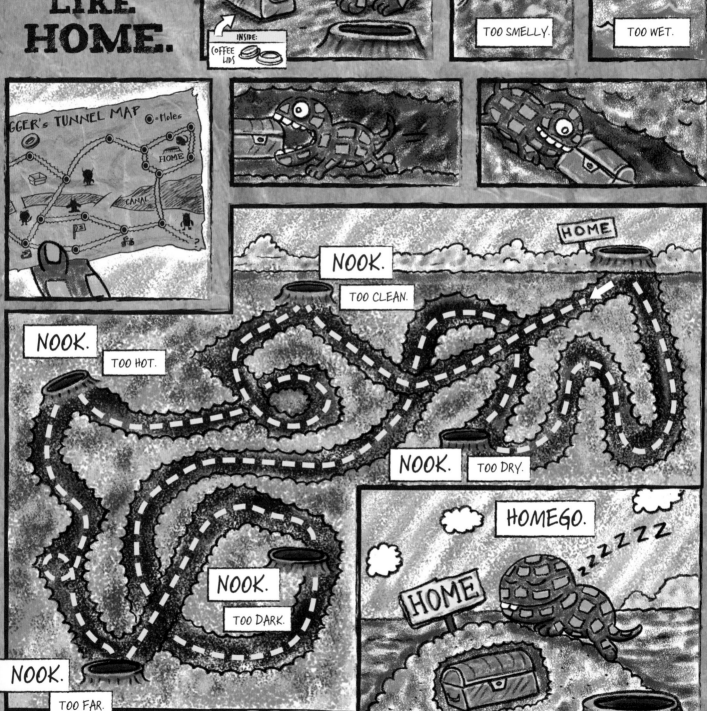

TREASURE CHEST

What You'll Need:

Cereal Box • Small Cardboard Tube • Pencil • Stapler • Paint • Paintbrush • Strong Tape • Ruler • String • Paper Clip • Hole Punch • Scissors • Markers & Crayons • Glue

1 Cut open cereal box. Cut off back and front panels.

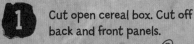

2 Use a ruler to draw a 4x3-inch rectangle in the middle of one panel.

A 3" 4"

Measure 1½ inches from each rectangle edge. Mark with pencil. Trim any extra cardboard.

B 1½"

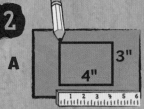

3 Make cuts at the four corners.

Fold up sides, with smaller tabs on outside. Staple.

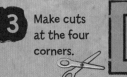

4 Cut open tube.

A

Measure 3 inches across the middle of other panel. Draw two lines.

B 3"

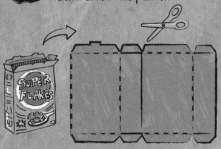

5 Place cut tube on cardboard so its edges touch lines. Trace the curved shape.

A

Draw a box at top of curve and one at each side. Cut out shape and trace it so you have two pieces.

B

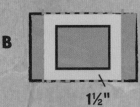 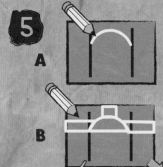

6 Fold tabs.

Staple tabs onto open tube at one edge. Repeat with other piece at opposite edge.

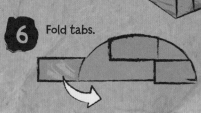 

7 Cut a small rectangle of cardboard. Staple one end inside the chest.

Tape other end inside the back wall of lid.

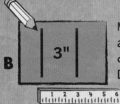 

8 Cut another small rectangle of cardboard. Cut off two corners. Staple to the inside front of lid. Punch a hole.

A

Put the paper clip on the front of chest with the smaller loop on the outside. Bend up bottom of loop.

B

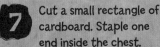  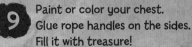

9 Paint or color your chest. Glue rope handles on the sides. Fill it with treasure!

DIGGER'S SECRET CODE

A B C | J K L
D E F | M N O
G H I | P Q R

S/T U/V | W/X Y/Z

Digger has invented a secret code to send messages to Itcher. Use the code to find the shape for each letter of the alphabet.

Here are a few examples. →

⌐ = A
⌐ = O
< = Y
□ = N
⋀ = V

CAN YOU CRACK DIGGER'S CODE?

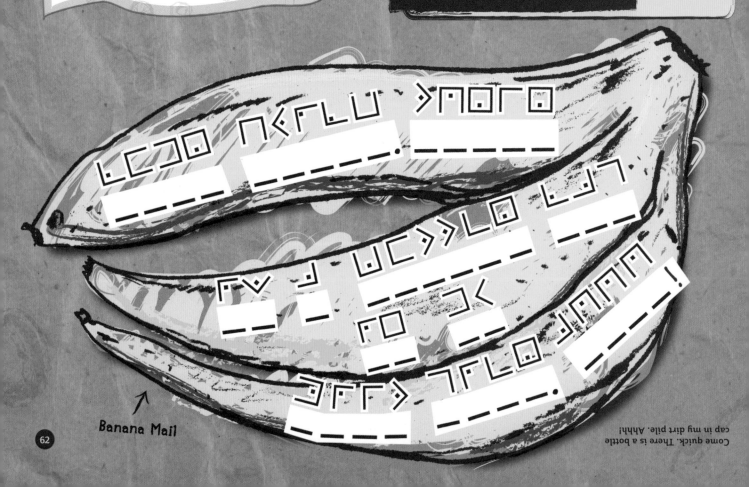

↖ Banana Mail

Come quick. There is a bottle cap in my dirt pile. Ahhh!

CODE BOOK

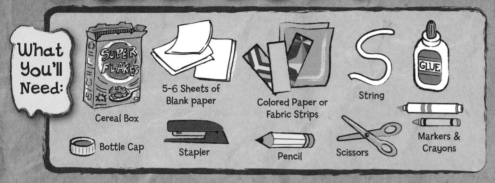

Cereal Box

5-6 Sheets of Blank paper

Colored Paper or Fabric Strips

String

GLUE

Bottle Cap

Stapler

Pencil

Scissors

Markers & Crayons

1 Cut off the front of the cereal box. Save the back for another journal.

2 Fold the cardboard in half, brown side facing out.

3 Stack the sheets of blank paper and fold the stack in half. Slide them inside the cover.

INSIDE PAGES

4 Line up the bottom edges of paper with the cover. Hold the paper in place and flip over the book.

Staple at the bottom, trim extra paper, then staple at the top.

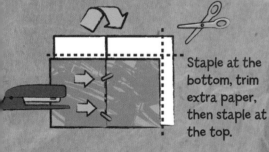

5 Cut a piece of colored paper or fabric to cover the spine of book. Glue it in place.

6 Trace bottle cap onto an extra piece of cardboard and cut it out.

7 Fold back the paper pages. Place the end of string on the front of book. Place the circle on top of the string end and staple it to front of book.

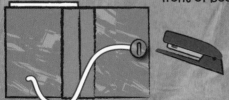

8 BE CREATIVE! Decorate your book!

9 Use your book to write secret notes to your friends using Digger's Code. When you close the book, wrap the string around the circle to keep it shut.

CASTLE GREEN

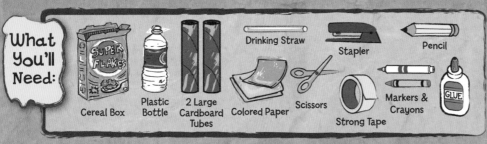

1 Unfold and flatten your cereal box. Cut the whole box in half. **TIP:** If you fold the box in half before cutting, it will be easier to make both sides the same height.

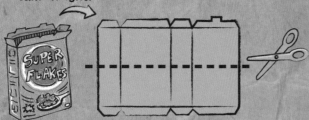

2 Turn the two pieces so the cut edges are at the **BOTTOM**, brown side up. Overlap the wide sections halfway and staple.

3 Draw a door shape in the center of the stapled area. Cut it out.

Cut the door shape into two pieces.

4 Trace the doors onto colored paper. Cut out the paper and glue onto doors.

5 Use a dark marker to draw rectangles and lines on your castle to make it look like bricks. Use crayons to color the walls.

Put a piece of strong tape on the back of each door and tape them inside the castle wall.

6 Fold up castle, overlapping the two small end pieces. Staple closed.

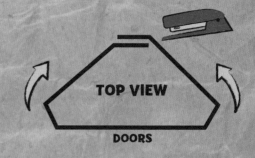

TOP VIEW

DOORS

7 Cut three small squares out of the top of each large tube. These are the towers. Color them green.

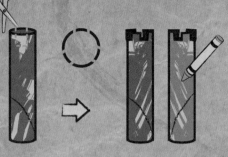

8 Insert the end of stapler between the edge of castle and the inside of tube. Staple in place.

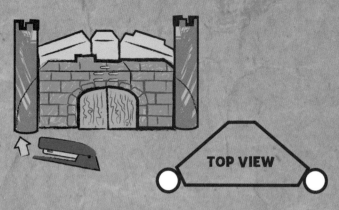

TOP VIEW

9 Cut off the top and bottom of plastic bottle. Gently push the bottom piece into the top. Secure with two staples if needed.

Cut two slits in the bottle from the bottom.

TOP VIEW

10 Slide the bottle onto the back middle flap.

11 Draw two flags on a piece of colored paper. Cut them out.

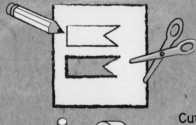

Cut a straw in half. Make a small cut in top of each straw half. Slide flag in each straw piece and tape on the back.

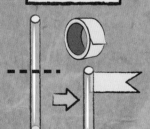

12 Cut two slits in the bottom of each straw and slide flags onto towers. Cut out a few squares from the walls to finish off your castle.

CHOMPER

MOP HEAD

SAW BLADE TEETH

I could EAT that!

He's a garbage disposal on legs. Chomper will eat anything!
DO NOT PUT STUFF NEAR HIS MOUTH. Crude, rebellious, and a practical joker, Chomper is obsessed with cooking. He spends hours creating new recipes and finding new ingredients. No one but Wrecks will try his cooking.

TOES & NAILS FOR OPENING CANS

TANGY SNEAKER STEW with LACES

INGREDIENTS: 3 Garlic Bulbs
12 Shoelaces
3 Rotten Eggs
Fistful of Batteries
1 Clump of Cut Grass
4 Sneakers (various sizes)
Pepper

1. Dice garlic and lightly fry shoelaces.
2. Mix eggs, batteries, and water in a giant pot. Boil mixture for ten minutes.
3. Sprinkle in grass and add sneakers one at a time until stew turns bright green. Stir in laces and grind in pepper to taste.

MISSION:

I baste, taste, and replace—
Bake and make meals out of stuff that you waste.
I eat day and night, biting through cans, hubcaps, spools of wire, and busted-up fans.
I make four-star meals while you're still making plans.

CHOMPER'S FRIDGE

Nuts & Bolts Pie

Mailbox Found in the Canal

Leftover Compost Stew with Chili Socks

MONSTER TRUCK

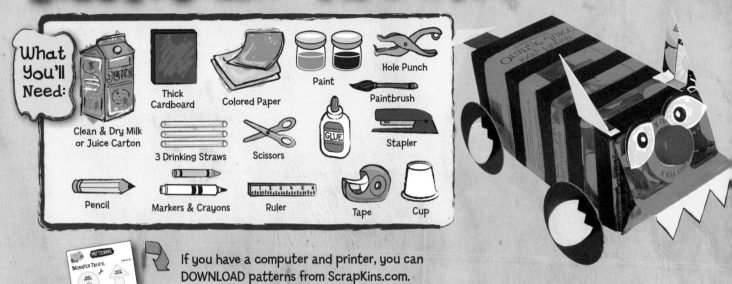

What You'll Need:

- Clean & Dry Milk or Juice Carton
- Thick Cardboard
- Colored Paper
- Paint
- Hole Punch
- Paintbrush
- 3 Drinking Straws
- Scissors
- GLUE
- Stapler
- Pencil
- Markers & Crayons
- Ruler
- Tape
- Cup

If you have a computer and printer, you can DOWNLOAD patterns from ScrapKins.com. But you don't need them to make the project.

1 **Ask an adult to help** cut off the bottom of carton.

Save this piece to use for your monster's features.

2 Paint the top carton piece. Set aside to dry.

3 Cut the four corners of carton bottom and fold flat.

Use the carton piece or colored paper to draw two eyes, a small triangle for the tail tip, a rectangle for the tail, and two triangles for horns. Cut them out with scissors.

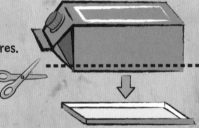

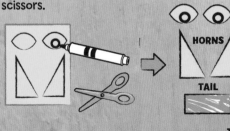

EYES

HORNS

TAIL

TAIL TIP

4 Trace a cup or something round (about 2½ inches across) onto cardboard. Cut out four wheels.

2½"

5 Punch a hole in the center of each wheel.

*If your hole puncher is too small to reach the center: Draw two crossing lines to help find the center of wheel. **Ask an adult to help** poke a hole through center of each wheel.

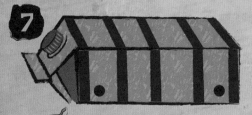

6

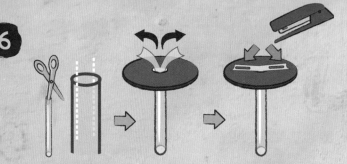

Cut two small slits in one end of two straws.

Insert end of straw through hole in wheel. Fold down ends of straw. Staple ends securely down. Repeat with other wheel.

7

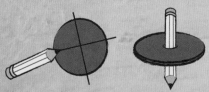

Punch two holes on each side of carton, close to bottom.

Insert a pencil into each hole and mark the inside edge. Punch holes on the other side using these marks. **TIP:** Use the pencil to make all the holes slightly bigger.

TOP VIEW

8

Fold up edge of horns and glue on top of carton. Staple triangle tail tip to one end of tail piece. Fold down back edge of tail piece. Insert stapler inside carton and staple tail on the back.

9 Insert open end of straw through hole in the carton. Trim extra straw off. *Leave about 1 inch of straw to attach other wheel.

Make two cuts in the end of straw, slide on other wheel, fold down straw ends, and staple.

10 Cut last straw in half. Slide one piece inside each of the axles. **TIP:** If the fit is too tight, cut open the straw along its edge.

11 Draw some teeth and four feet on paper.

FOOT

TEETH

Cut them out.

12 Glue eyes on front.

Tape teeth on front edge.

Staple feet over the straw ends on wheels.

69

INVENT A PIZZA

CHOMPER NEEDS TO MAKE A NEW PIZZA FOR HIS RESTAURANT, THE LEFTOVERS CAFÉ. GET CREATIVE! CAN YOU DESIGN A PIZZA THE WORLD HAS NEVER SEEN?

Hurry up.
I'm hungry!

PIZZA NAME:

Oc-Tube-Pus

1 Cut out a semicircle mouth shape from top of tube.

2

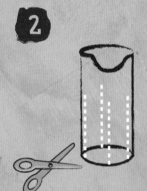

Make four cuts in tube to halfway up tube.

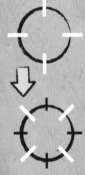

Make four more cuts in tube, between the first cuts. These will be the tentacles.

3 Bend out the tentacles. Round off corners.

4 Cut off one cup from an egg carton. Trim edges so that it is round.

5 Glue carton cup onto top of tube. Set aside to dry.

6 When glue is dry, paint your oc-tube-pus.

When paint is dry, draw two eyes on paper and cut out. Glue them on the head.

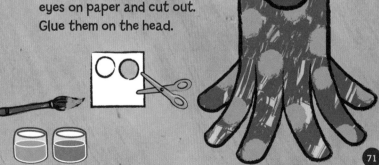

CHOMPER IN . . .

SLOP, GURGLE, POP!

CHOMPER FINDS A CASE OF SODA. . . .

WHATCHA DOING, CHOMPER?

WRECKS! JOIN ME IN AN EXPERIMENT I'M DOING.

GURGLE GURGLE

READY FOR OUR FIRST TEST!

BRAAP!

RUURRP!

HA! HA!

HEH! HEH!

WATCH THIS.

BURBY

BRAAPP!

FIRE BELCH!

I HAVE AN IDEA.

READY! SET! . . .

LEANING TOWER OF PIZZA BOXES (184 FEET)

BRAAAAAB BA BOOM!

REMIND ME NOT TO LET YOU BURP IN PUBLIC.

EXCUSE ME.

CHOMPER CLAWS

What You'll Need:

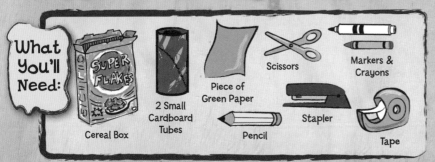

- Cereal Box
- 2 Small Cardboard Tubes
- Piece of Green Paper
- Scissors
- Markers & Crayons
- Pencil
- Stapler
- Tape

1 Unfold and flatten your cereal box. Draw a U shape bigger than your hand. Cut out. Trace it and cut out another.

2 Draw a claw shape with three points. You can use the U shape to help with the size. Cut out a claw, then trace it and cut out another.

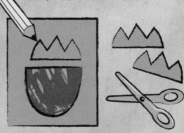

3 Color the hand shapes blue.

4 Flatten tube. Cut in half. Repeat with other tube.

5 Turn over hand shapes and tape on claws.

6 Place two of the tube pieces on top of one hand and staple in place next to each other. Repeat with the other tube pieces on the other hand.

7 Slide your fingers into the tubes so they cover your hands.

Now you have Chomper Claws!

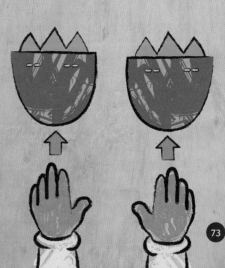

BALLOON RACER

What You'll Need:

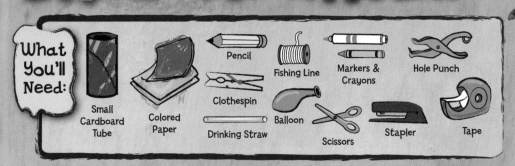

- Small Cardboard Tube
- Colored Paper
- Pencil
- Fishing Line
- Markers & Crayons
- Hole Punch
- Clothespin
- Drinking Straw
- Balloon
- Scissors
- Stapler
- Tape

1 Flatten tube.

2 Design and decorate the tube like a rocket.

3 Cut out fins or other shapes for your racer. Attach with tape or staple.

4 Cut straw in half.

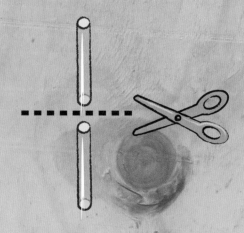

5 Use two pieces of tape to attach straw piece to top of tube.

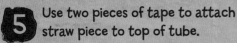

6 Attach one end of fishing line to a wall or chair. Thread line through the straw and pull tight. Tape end of line to another chair or wall.

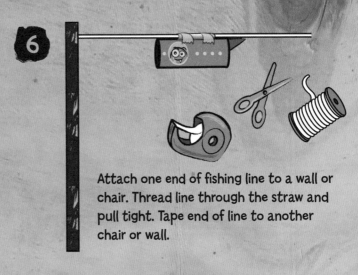

7 Blow up balloon and place clothespin over the opening.

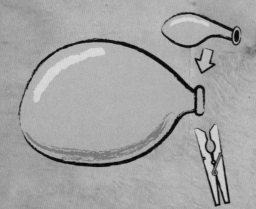

8 Make two loops of tape with the sticky side outside. Place them on top of balloon and stick to the bottom of tube. Press firmly to make sure they hold together.

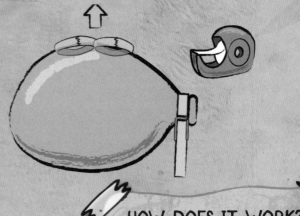

9 Remove the clothespin while pinching the opening of the balloon. Give a countdown: 3, 2, 1, then let go!

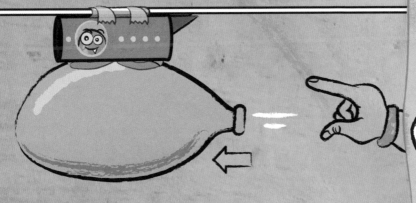

HOW DOES IT WORK?

The **AIR** trapped inside the balloon is under pressure. When you release the opening, the air wants to escape to lower the pressure, and it all rushes out. The **FORCE** of the air escaping in one direction (backward) pushes the racer the other direction (forward).

What happens when you blow up the balloon **BIGGER**?

HOW to DRAW ITCHER

1

2

3

4

5

6

7

8

HOW to DRAW SWOOPER

1

2

3

4

5

6

7

HOW to DRAW STACKER

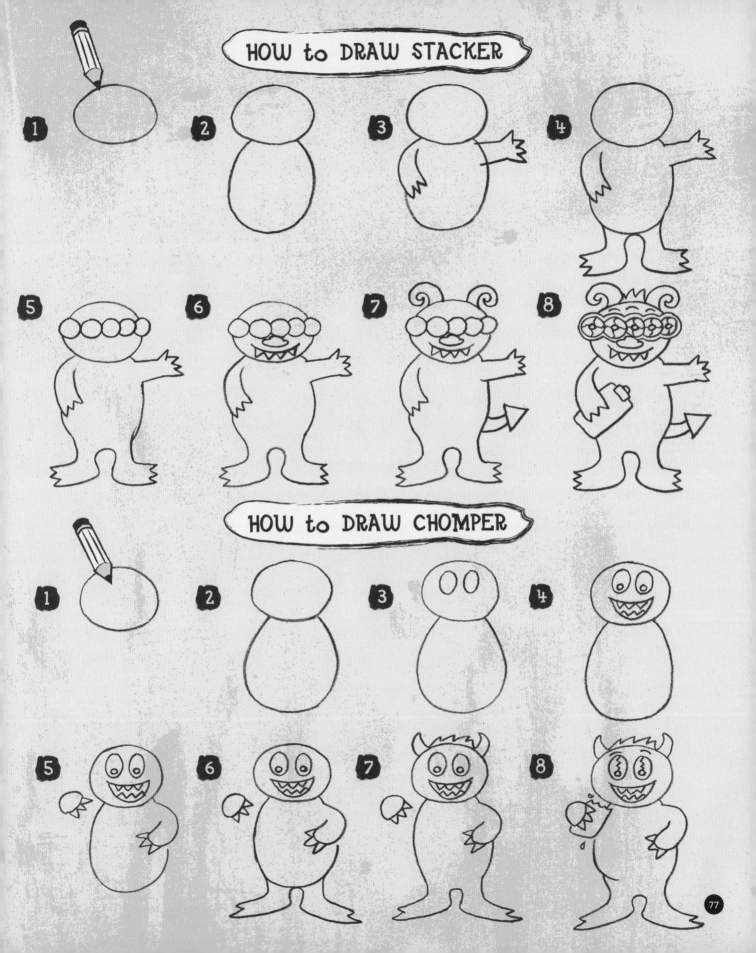

1 **2** **3** **4**

5 **6** **7** **8**

HOW to DRAW CHOMPER

1 **2** **3** **4**

5 **6** **7** **8**

77

HOW to DRAW DIGGER

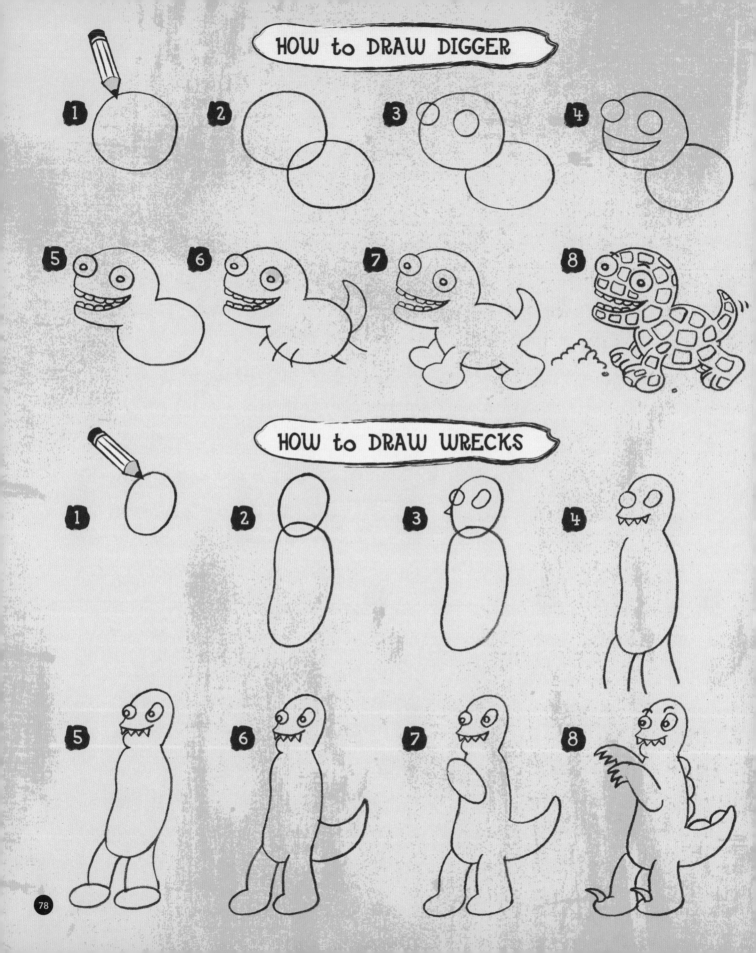

1
2
3
4
5
6
7
8

HOW to DRAW WRECKS

1
2
3
4
5
6
7
8

Scrap Kins

BRIAN YANISH is a professional illustrator. He has worked for Jim Henson Productions in Los Angeles, trained as a special effects mold maker, written and performed comedy, designed educational software, and sold his own line of T-shirts. He currently lives in New York City, where he writes and illustrates children's books and designs and develops stories and characters for live events, museums, television, toys, apps, and other media.

THE ULTIMATE RECYCLING PROJECT

ScrapKins started from a love of drawing and making things. As a child, I spent hours drawing creatures and building gifts and tiny creations in my father's home workshop. Many years later, my mother handed me a folder containing all my childhood drawings. That's when I created the world of ScrapKins and cast my original characters as the heroes of their own adventures, living in a world of discarded items full of possibility. The ScrapKins have inspired thousands of kids to find creativity in common materials.

Brian's childhood drawings of the Scrapkins, 1980

Itcher

Swooper

Stacker

scrapkins.com

© Alejandro Cerdena Photography

© Alejandro Cerdena Photography

© Drew B. Photography